This book belongs to . . .

_____

MARTY
the
MARMOT

by
Joe Maniscalco

Published by Southern Publishing Association, Nashville, Tennessee

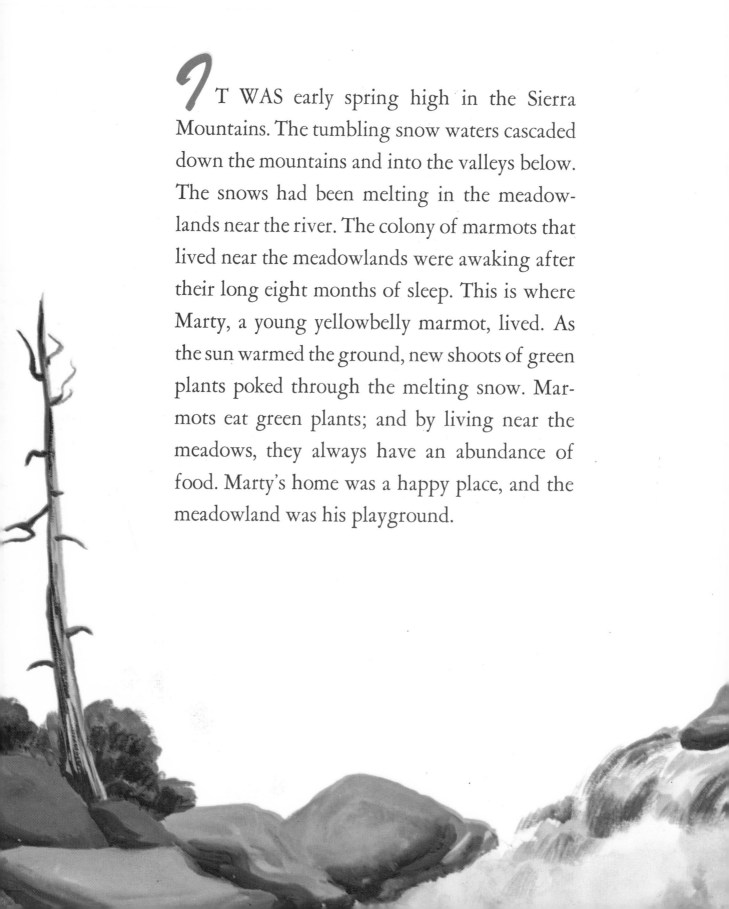

*I*T WAS early spring high in the Sierra Mountains. The tumbling snow waters cascaded down the mountains and into the valleys below. The snows had been melting in the meadowlands near the river. The colony of marmots that lived near the meadowlands were awaking after their long eight months of sleep. This is where Marty, a young yellowbelly marmot, lived. As the sun warmed the ground, new shoots of green plants poked through the melting snow. Marmots eat green plants; and by living near the meadows, they always have an abundance of food. Marty's home was a happy place, and the meadowland was his playground.

*I*T WAS the month of May, and the marmot colony was busy repairing its burrows. Many of the tunnels had caved in and had to be cleared. Marmots must work together in order to survive the many dangers that lurk about them. A sentinel marmot was selected to be on the lookout for danger. He sat on a high boulder with his ears and eyes ever on the alert. When danger threatened, the sentinel marmot gave out a high-pitched whistle, and the colony of marmots·dived into their burrows, where they were safe from their enemies.

A SHARP EYE must be kept on the look-out for King Cat, the mountain lion. He had a hungry family in the rimrock cave above the meadowland. He often prowled near the marmot colony at night and sometimes would wait until morning to try to catch a marmot off guard. He was strong and fast, and able to leap twenty feet in one easy bound. When he was near the marmot colony, the sentinel marmot was keenly alert, ready to give the alarm at the first sign of danger. When King Cat was seen, a shrill whistle broke the silence, and the marmot colony disappeared.

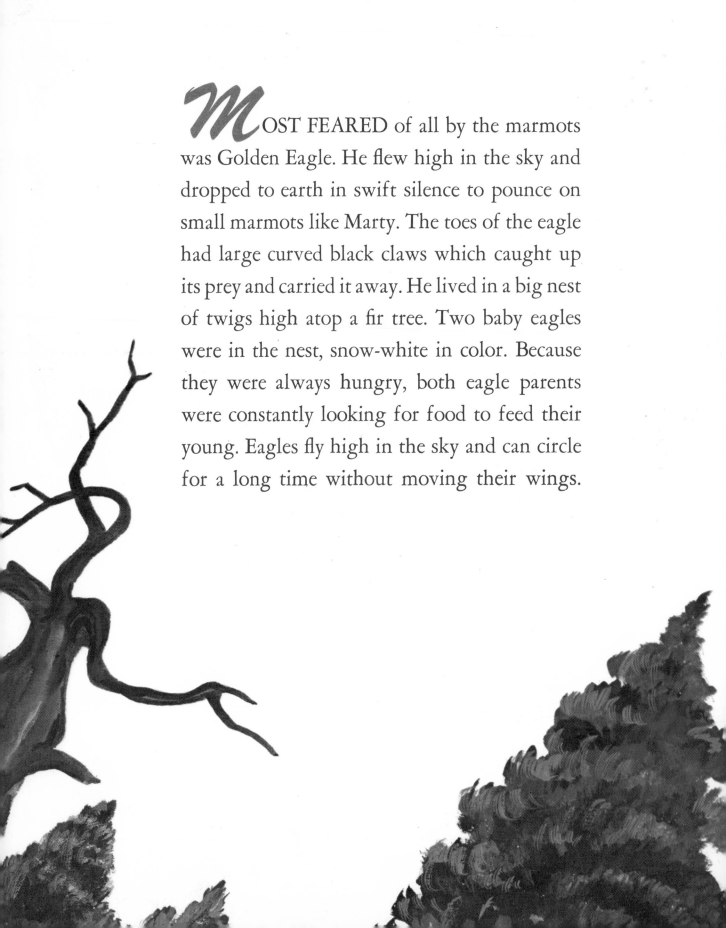

M OST FEARED of all by the marmots was Golden Eagle. He flew high in the sky and dropped to earth in swift silence to pounce on small marmots like Marty. The toes of the eagle had large curved black claws which caught up its prey and carried it away. He lived in a big nest of twigs high atop a fir tree. Two baby eagles were in the nest, snow-white in color. Because they were always hungry, both eagle parents were constantly looking for food to feed their young. Eagles fly high in the sky and can circle for a long time without moving their wings.

$\mathcal{M}$ARTY HAD been warned about such enemies, but he was young and delighted in exploring the great wilderness near his home. His curiosity led him away from the safety of the meadow and into the deep forest. He saw the large fir and pine trees that grew high into the sky. A game trail wound through the woods beside a river. Marty decided to explore the trail and wandered farther and farther away from his meadowland colony. It was not long before Marty was far out of sight of the safety of his home.

$\mathcal{M}$ARTY WALKED around a bend of the river and near it discovered a strange creature. This little animal did not move or speak. He was covered with spots and had two big ears. Marty walked up to the little animal and sniffed, but did not smell anything different. Soon a mother deer hurried up to investigate the little snooper. Marty was friendly, so she did not hurt him, but wandered away through the woods with her baby close behind.

$\mathcal{M}$ARTY CONTINUED to follow the trail. It led him to a large lake. Looking up, his sharp little eyes noticed Osprey, the fish hawk. The black shadow circled high in the sky and suddenly darted down into the water and came up with a fish. High overhead Marty noticed another dark shadow. It was Baldy, the eagle. The eagle plummeted toward Osprey, who wisely dropped his fish to seek safety in flight. Baldy dived after the fish, catching it in midair, and flew off to his nest. Osprey was a good fisherman and would soon catch another fish for his dinner.

VENTURESOME MARTY soon learned that this large lake was a place of strange sights and adventure. Thirsty for a drink, the little marmot walked to the water's edge. While drinking, Marty noticed that two long sticks moved. Looking up, he found a long-beaked bird roosting atop the sticks. It was Great Blue Heron waiting patiently for a fish. Suddenly he poked his bill into the water and tossed a fish into the air, catching it headfirst. This allowed him to swallow the fish without catching the fins in his long throat. What a smart bird! thought Marty, as he wandered on around the lake.

SINCE MARTY was hungry, he ate the new shoots of grass coming up along the lake's edge. He would stand on his hind legs and reach as high as his little body would go and pluck at the green tips of the pine needles. They tasted good to a young exploring marmot. Marty ate and ate until he was full. Now if he could find a warm stone to lie on, he would take a nap. After a short search, Marty found a nice smooth stone. He stretched out on it and was soon fast asleep.

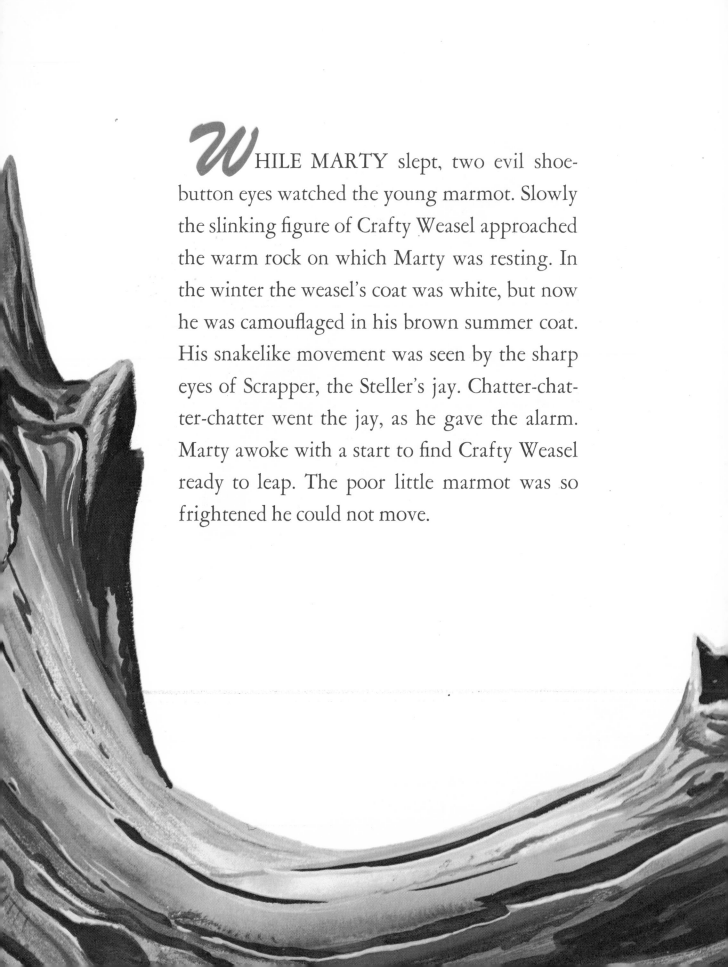

WHILE MARTY slept, two evil shoe-button eyes watched the young marmot. Slowly the slinking figure of Crafty Weasel approached the warm rock on which Marty was resting. In the winter the weasel's coat was white, but now he was camouflaged in his brown summer coat. His snakelike movement was seen by the sharp eyes of Scrapper, the Steller's jay. Chatter-chatter-chatter went the jay, as he gave the alarm. Marty awoke with a start to find Crafty Weasel ready to leap. The poor little marmot was so frightened he could not move.

UNKNOWN TO MARTY, Tuffy, the skunk, was sleeping in the shade of the smooth rock. Up flew his tail, and a fine spray struck Crafty Weasel in the eyes. Off he ran, stumbling through the woods. He would not stalk little marmots for many days to come. Tuffy was a striped skunk that lived in a hollow log near the tree where Scrapper, the Steller's jay, had his nest. He walked with his tail up, proudly waving it as he strolled through the woods. Marty was very grateful that Tuffy Skunk was nearby to save him from Crafty Weasel.

MARTY NEEDED a drink of water after his narrow escape from Crafty Weasel. As he started to walk toward the water, he suddenly heard a splash. Marty wondered what made that splash. Looking toward the water, he saw an animal that looked as if he were wearing a mask. He had a fluffy tail with black rings on it. It was a hungry raccoon that had just caught a crayfish for his evening meal. Raccoons love water and are never too far from a lake or river. Marty noticed that he washed his food before he ate it. His front paws, like tiny hands, handled his food very carefully. Marty thought raccoons were clean animals, to wash their food before they ate it.

$\mathcal{M}$ARMOTS SLEEP in their burrows at the close of the day. Now the sun was almost set. Marty kept looking for a place to sleep. The moon was full, making it possible for Marty to see. Finally he found an old hollow log. This would be a fine place for a young marmot to spend the night. Marty was about to crawl into the hollow log when he heard, "Whoo-hoo-hoo." Looking up, Marty saw a horned owl. He was big, and his feet had large claws. Down flew the owl, and Marty was surprised that he could not hear his wings flap. The owl was hungry for mice. Marty crawled into the hollow log and was soon fast asleep.

WHEN MARTY awoke from his sleep, the sun was shining brightly. After eating some of the green plants near the lake, he decided to walk along the water's edge. Splash, splash, splash—what could be making that noise? At the far end of the lake, Marty noticed three otters sliding down a slippery bank. They wet their bodies and climbed up on the high bank. Down they slid headfirst into the water. Otters seem to play most of the time and are the funny family of the woods. They are well suited to life in the water. The four feet are webbed, and their bodies are streamlined. Marty thought that he would like to be an otter and be able to slide into the water.

$\mathcal{M}$ARTY THOUGHT it was time to head for home. He wondered how he could get across the lake without having to go back around the way he had come. The lake was getting narrower as Marty walked along the bank. He noticed a dam that crossed the narrow edge of the lake. It was made of large sticks and had mud on its top. He wondered what made that dam. Splash! went a tree as it tumbled into the water. There at the base was a beaver; this was a beaver dam. Marty saw beavers working all over the dam. Beavers worked together and swam in the deep clear pools of water. Marty crossed the dam and ran toward home.

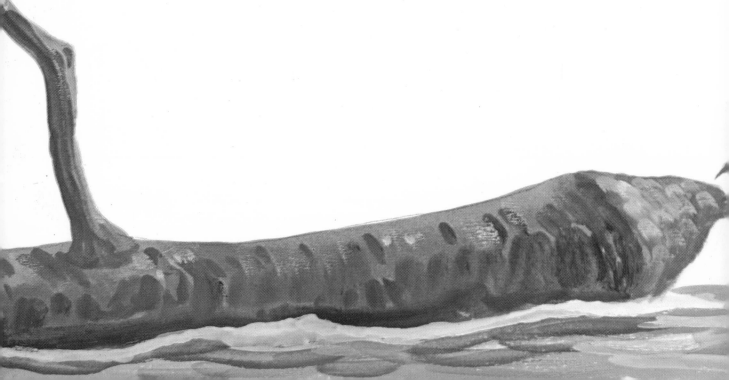

MARTY RAN so fast he was soon home. All the marmot colony was happy to see him. He was scolded by his mother and told not to wander away from home again. Marty was happy to be home and to know that the sentinel marmot was nearby to warn of danger. He played and lived happily in the marmot colony all summer. He found many hiding places; an old hollow tree near a rockslide was his favorite. His friend Yellow Hair, the porcupine, often climbed the tree. Marty liked his friend the porcupine but thought he made too much noise when he ate the bark toward the bottom of the tree. He was a slow-moving animal, but did not have to worry about enemies; his sharp quills kept them away.

SOON THE SUMMER was over, and the sky was heavy with clouds. Marty noticed that the days were not as sunny and warm as they used to be. The birds' songs were much quieter. Overhead he noticed a big V in the sky. The Canada geese were honking their way toward the south. Then one cold evening the patient old fisherman Mr. Great Blue Heron headed south over the dark trees. Many animals were preparing to enter their winter homes. Marty felt that the meadowland was getting to be a lonely place.

$\mathcal{M}$ARTY BECAME very sleepy about the time the first flakes of snow began to fall. He crawled down into a burrow and curled up into a ball in a snug grassy room. The entrance of his burrow was closed with dirt, and Marty fell fast asleep for the long winter months. His friend the chipmunk was asleep, and Mr. Black Bear had found a cave in which to sleep. The snow clouds hung heavy over the meadowland, and soon the marmot colony was covered with a thick layer of clean white snow.

…and that is the story of Marty the Marmot and his adventures high in the Sierra Mountains.